Simon Boulerice has always loved to dance, act and write. Based in Montreal, Quebec, he is a playwright, a poet and the award-winning author of several books for children and adults. He has been called one of the most original voices in our generation, and at the age of thirty-five, he still does the splits at least once a day.

Delphie Côté-Lacroix is a multidisciplinary visual artist with a background in graphic design. *Florence & Léon* (QuébecAmérique) was a finalist for the 2016 Governor General's Award for Children's Illustration (French). She lives and works out of Montreal, Quebec. For more information, visit delphiecotelacroix.com.

Florence & Leon

Simon Boulerice

Delphie Côté-Lacroix

Translated from the French by Sophie B. Watson

ORCA BOOK PUBLISHERS

Cataloguing in Publication information available from Library and Archives Canada

Issued in print and electronic formats.
ISBN 978-1-4598-1822-4 (hardcover).—ISBN 978-1-4598-1823-1 (pdf).—
ISBN 978-1-4598-1824-8 (epub)

First published in the United States, 2018
Library of Congress Control Number: 2018933709

Summary: A touching story about a friendship where differences become strengths and the length of a straw brings two people together.

Orca Book Publishers is dedicated to preserving the environment and has printed this book on Forest Stewardship Council® certified paper.

Orca Book Publishers gratefully acknowledges the support for its publishing programs provided by the following agencies: the Government of Canada through the Canada Book Fund and the Canada Council for the Arts, and the Province of British Columbia through the BC Arts Council and the Book Publishing Tax Credit.

We acknowledge the financial support of the Government of Canada through the National Translation Program for Book Publishing, an initiative of the *Roadmap for Canada's Official Languages 2013-2018: Education, Immigration, Communities,* for our translation activities.

Artwork created using watercolor, colored pencil and graphite and digital editing.
Cover and interior artwork by Delphie Côté-Lacroix
Translated by Sophie B. Watson

ORCA BOOK PUBLISHERS
orcabook.com

Printed and bound in Canada.

21 20 19 18 • 4 3 2 1

To Méridick Forest, who made
me see the world differently.

—S.B.

As a child, when Florence went swimming she often found herself a whole lap ahead of her friend Constance.

As a reward, her mother used to buy her a slushy drink from the corner store. Florence always chose to drink it through a bendy straw full of twists and turns. Florence knew she'd grow up to be a colorful woman. A *Florence full of flair*.

99¢

When Leon was a young boy, competing
with his friend Simon on the soccer pitch,
sometimes he would end up diving sideways
to the ground with the length of his whole
body—in the absolutely wrong direction!

To console himself when he returned home, he would pour himself a big glass of mango and melon juice. He would drink it with a superlong straw that stretched to infinity. Leon knew he'd become a tall man one day. A *long Leon*.

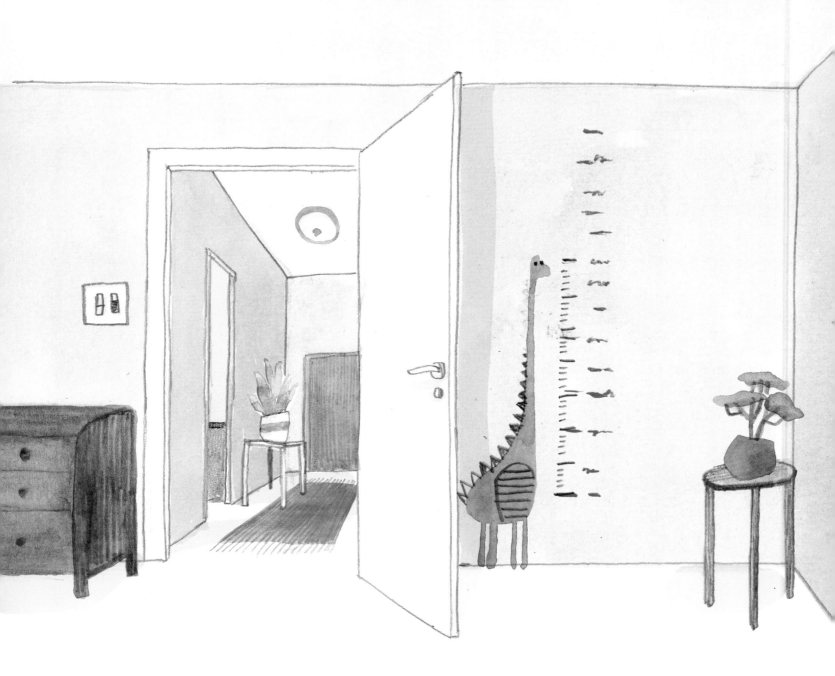

Now Florence has left her childhood behind
her, and Leon is almost as tall as the ceiling.
They have become adults.

Florence gives swimming lessons. She teaches children how to hold their breath underwater.

Leon is an insurance agent. He sells assurances to people who want to ensure everything will go well when things go wrong.

They don't know each other yet.
But today their lives will change.
Today they will collide.

Like always, Florence is in a hurry. She is
breathless and worried about being late.
She doesn't look where she puts her feet and
trips on a young man's cane. It's Leon.

Florence falls backward. And Leon collapses. The swimming teacher muddles through an apology.

I'm sorry, sir.
I didn't see you!

Not to worry! I didn't see you either. I have a small problem with my eyes!

Florence looks at Leon's cane. A white cane with a red end. She doesn't know what to say. Faced with his confession, she decides to make her own, to make it equal between them.

Well, I have some small lung problems myself!

There they are, both of them on the ground, giggling, helping each other to get back up. Their encounter has been as honest as could be—they have talked about their disabilities even before sharing their names.

Once they have gotten their introductions out of the way, Leon suggests they go get something to drink to treat themselves. But the young woman can't go right then, because children in swimsuits are waiting for her. The two strangers make a plan to meet in an hour at the corner café.

Patiently Leon waits alone at the café until Florence's class is finished. When she arrives, fifteen minutes late, he notices the perfume of her skin—a mixture of vanilla and chlorine. People who have problems with their eyes often have a superior sense of smell.

"When one sense weakens, another sharpens," Leon explains to the swimming teacher. "My ears are also impressive," he adds. "I recognized your footsteps before seeing you!"

"You're lucky!" Florence says. "My ears are always plugged with pool water."

Leon drinks a glass of mango and melon juice. Florence fancies a slushy drink, but there aren't any. She chooses an iced coffee. Each of their straws is nice and straight, certainly not twisty or stretchable. After all, Florence and Leon are proper adults now.

Sitting there, they tell each other the story of their lives—their jobs, their childhoods and their peculiarities. Florence asks him if he can see all of her.

"No," he replies. "I can only see a tiny sliver of you."

What about if I move slightly and sit here. Do you see me at all?

Yes, a tiny bit.

And if I'm over here?

Barely at all.

And here?

Only one strand of hair.

And here?

No.

Florence takes advantage of his little eye problem by sneaking
a peek at his profile. Why not? He can't tell she's doing it.
What a handsome man! And elegant too, she tells herself.

Florence uses her straw to slurp up the very last of her iced coffee. The gesture makes Leon smile as he explains his vision problems.

"It's as if I'm always looking through a little cylinder. In fact, I see you exactly as you would see me through your straw."

Florence immediately positions her straw, with no bends or twists, nice and straight in front of her eye. All she can see is Leon's smile. She moves the straw around and sees a nose, then an eye and then another eye.

"So you don't see all of me?"

"Yes and no. Fortunately, my brain puts all your pieces together like a puzzle."

"So you don't know if I'm pretty or not?"

"I'd have to be completely blind to not see that you are pretty!"

Florence's face turns red as a poppy.

To mask her embarrassment,
she starts chatting—a lot.

"I don't like my rib cage. I have always found it to be too big. That's because of my lung problems. Lungs are in charge of filling up rib cages. My lungs are always searching for air. When I was small, my swimming teacher wanted to explain my condition to my classmates. To make them understand what was happening in my lungs, he had them run for three minutes around the school and then breathe through a straw. Needless to say, my classmates were better able to understand the challenge that swimming the length of a pool meant for me with my demanding lungs."

Leon listens to Florence with tenderness but also with a little envy and regret. He explains, "My phys ed teacher found it funny, my vision problems. He said nothing when I got a ball in the face, even when my classmates were aiming it directly at me."

Florence brings her hand to her mouth, upset by how mean his classmates had been.

Leon brushes away the memory with a wave of his hand and stands up.

"My turn to try your straw trick," he exclaims.

"But you might hurt yourself. It must be dangerous to run with your cane!"

"So I will run on the spot!"

The insurance agent starts hopping up and down in front of Florence. All the other customers look at him with either mild annoyance or puzzlement, but Leon doesn't care. He can't see them!

Florence laughs her heart out at the spectacle of her new friend skipping up and down in front of her. After three minutes Leon, out of breath, removes the straw from his juice and tries his best to breathe through it. He struggles to get enough air. He turns red as a beet.

And here they are, Florence and Leon, with their straws, beaming at each other, red as flowers and vegetables.

Florence is happy that her straw is nice and straight. She never would have been able to look at the insurance agent through a bendy straw.

Leon, well, he is happy that his straw doesn't stretch. He never would have been able to breathe like the swimming teacher through a straw that was too long. Plus an extra-long straw would keep him far from her.

Leon would like to get closer to Florence.

And Florence would like that too.

Time passes, and then they have to go their separate ways, returning to their own homes. They promise to see each other as soon as possible.

Tomorrow perhaps?

Yes, why not? Tomorrow.

Outside there is heavy traffic. Car horns are making a terrible racket. At the intersection it is taking a very long time for the crosswalk light to turn green. Florence has an idea. With a delightfully focused look, she blows in the direction of the red hand. On cue, the light transforms into the walking pedestrian.

You're a magician, you are!

A little.

But Florence is surprised. Can Leon see the little green man from so far away?

"No, but I hear the signal noise that tells me we can cross. My hearing is sharp."

"I can't hear anything. It must be all that pool water."

Florence offers Leon her arm to cross the road. They feel comfortable together.

I offer to be your ears.

Perfect! And I will be your eyes.

For the rest of the day?

Why not forever?

Indeed, why not?